KT-424-112

Llyfrgelloedd Caerdydd
www.caerdydd.gov.uk/llyfrgelloedd
Cardiff Libraries
www.cardiff.gov.uk/libraries

CAERDYDD
CARDIFF

ACC. No: 07048709

For Mark, with love ~ T C

For Laura and my family, thanks for all the
positive vibes and support ~ T N

LITTLE TIGER PRESS LTD,
an imprint of the Little Tiger Group
1 Coda Studios,
189 Munster Road,
London SW6 6AW
www.littletiger.co.uk

First published in Great Britain 2019

Text copyright © Tracey Corderoy 2019
Illustrations copyright © Tony Neal 2019
Tracey Corderoy and Tony Neal have asserted their rights
to be identified as the author and illustrator of this work
under the Copyright, Designs and Patents Act, 1988
A CIP catalogue record for this book is available
from the British Library

All rights reserved • ISBN 978-1-78881-100-2
Printed in China • LTP/1400/2360/0918

2 4 6 8 10 9 7 5 3 1

THE ONE-STOP
STORY SHOP

Tracey Corderoy

Tony Neal

LITTLE TIGER

LONDON

Once upon a time,
in a deep, dark forest, a fearless
knight came to slay a terrible dragon.
"Come out and meet your match, you great
big beastie!" hollered the knight.

He swished his sword, but there was no fiery roar.
So he tiptoed closer and closer . . .

Then the knight saw a note.
A note from the dragon.

Dear Mr Fearless Knight,
I've gone on holiday
for some "me" time.
Back in two weeks.
Love,
The Terrible Dragon
x

"Botheration!"
boomed the knight.
"Gone on holiday?! How can I finish my
adventure? With no dragon, my story
is STUCK!"

"Stuck?"
said a neighbour,
overhearing.
"Follow me!"
And she led him
to a shop.

"The One-Stop
Story Shop,"
the knight read.
"Wigs, wands,
characters, plots
and MORE."
It sounded perfect!
So in he went.

"I'm in need of a
dragon,"
announced the knight.
"The **feistiest** one
you have."

"Oh dear," said the
shopkeeper. "We've
sold out of dragons.
But if feisty is what
you're after, I have
JUST the thing."

"Ta-daaaa!"

"A ferret?!"
gasped the knight.
"He's **fluffy**, not feisty.
Whoever heard of a knight
slaying a **ferret?**"

"Hey, I can be really feisty!"
the ferret beamed.

The shopkeeper nodded. "Of course knights
slay ferrets! We just need the right story."
He checked his drawers and cupboards
crammed with tales just **bursting** to be told.
"Aha!" he said. "Maybe something like . . ."

"...The Starry Space Chase Adventure.
First, you zoom far across the galaxy.
Then you slay the – wait for it! –

Space Ferret
of DOOM!"

"No, no, you **nincompoop!**" blustered the knight. "Knights don't fly spaceships. They ride gallant horses."

"Well," said the shopkeeper, "if it's **horses** you want, then how about . . ."

" . . . The Hold-On-to-Your-Hats **Cowboy Adventure.** Here you'll hunt down **Wild Will Ferret,** the meanest outlaw in town."

But the cowboy horse was a **bonkers** buckaroo.

"Slow down!" bellowed the knight, bumping about.

"Woaahhh!"

Perhaps this tale wasn't quite right either.

"Let's try my **Story of the Month,**" said the shopkeeper. "At half price, you're **SURE** to enjoy . . ."

"...The Rumble-in-the-Jungle Explorer Adventure!
Includes elephants, bug spray and treasure map."
"Oh, yes!" cried the knight, brightening
at once. "Knights LOVE treasure."
"So do ferrets!" whooped Ferret.
"Off on our quest at last!"

But someone **else** was keen to sneak along too . . .

"G-goodness, thank you!" spluttered the knight.
"Even knights sometimes need their—"

"Friends?" suggested Ferret.

"Why . . . yes," the knight
nodded. "Their friends."

They rested a while,
and all was calm until – SPLAT!

"Bird poo?!"
scowled the knight.
"Mr Shopkeeper,
please find us a
PROPER adventure!"

"With some water to wash off
the poo," added Ferret.

"Hmm, water . . ." said the
shopkeeper. "Let me see."
He opened a hatch
and down they all
dived to . . .

. . . The Deep Dark Ocean Adventure.
"Why, this story has it all!" exclaimed the
knight. "Gallant horses, a mysterious cave
and treasure galore. Now we just need
a terrible beastie to fight. Isn't
that right, Ferret?

Ferret?!"

"Drop that ferret!!"
commanded the knight.
His moment for
battle had come
at last.

"Charge!"
he roared, off to save his friend.

And he fought
long
and
hard,

until Ferret was free!

"Hurrah for us!"
cheered the knight.
"We did it!"

But back came the beastie,
wild with rage.

"Quick!!"
called the knight.
"There must be
something that
will stop him!"

Ferret looked
high and low.
"A plug!!"
He grabbed the chain,
pulled hard and . . .

WHOOOOOSH!

. . . the beast
was gone!

"What a splendid adventure!" twinkled the knight.
"From now on, Ferret, you will always be by my side."
"Gosh, really?!" gasped Ferret.
But then a voice called . . .

"yoo-hoo!"

It was the dragon, back early from his holiday.
"The weather was absolutely AWFUL!" he puffed.
"Shall we have that battle now, Mr Knight?"

"No thanks!" chuckled the knight.
"I'm done with dragons. There's a whole
world of stories just waiting for
me and Ferret!"

And off they galloped into the sunset
to find their next thrilling adventure.